To Andrew

Kikitu Saves *Christmas*

Best Wishes   Tommy Conner

by

Tommy Conner

Illustrations by
Natalia Starikova

For Stephanie
Always

CHAPTER ONE

Tongues hung out of gaping mouths as they gasped for air. Feet pounded in rhythm in the frozen white wilderness of snow. The sled dog team worked in unison, as Yuka urged them on.

"Hike! Hike! Keep going. We need to be home for Christmas," she called from the back of the sled.

"Kik, take the best path. You know the way."

Yuka and Kikitu had been together for what seemed like forever. Yuka's grandfather had presented her with the white pup in a binding ceremony witnessed by the whole village when she was a young girl of five. Now Kikitu was six and fully grown and very strong.

1

Grandfather Jaekwan was the band leader for the Inuit village. On special occasions, the spirits moved him to join animals with humans as guardians to each other. So it was that the dog never left Yuka's side.

It was said Kikitu pulled Yuka from the frozen water when she fell in. He had also fought the great white bear that had tried to attack her and guided her home when she was lost.

Pure white with bright-blue azure eyes, no one knew for sure what breed of dog Kikitu was. He could be part husky and part Alaskan Malamute. But most thought that because of his size, strength, and stamina for running he was also part wolf.

They had been out long enough. Now Yuka wanted to be home with family and friends. Her grandfather was old, but full of life. He led the dance of the silver moon when the tribe was together, and he told stories of olden days when their people had to live off the land and sea. He shared tales of when clothing was made from animal skins. To soften the skins, they had to chew and chew and chew them until they were soft enough to stich together. The women made *amauti*, parkas with large hoods to carry babies on their backs. It wasn't like today. Now you can order online all sorts of winter gear like snowsuits, socks, boots, mitts, hats, and snow goggles.

Yuka shielded her eyes and looked into the morning sky. It looked like a star was coming straight towards them. As it got closer and closer, she could see white lights burning from the front and a glow of colours surrounding it.

"Whoa!" Yuka called out, and they all slithered to a stop. All eight dogs and Yuka were mesmerized by the ball speeding towards them, faster and faster. It grew in size the closer it got. The dogs started yelping, and Yuka did not know how to get out of the way since it was coming directly at them. The right dogs tried to run to the right, and the left tried to run to the left. In the panic and confusion, dogs jumped up and down and over one another. Harnesses tangled up, and some dogs fell over. Some landed on top, while others were trapped underneath.

The girl could only stare with an open mouth. Yuka felt like her body had been struck motionless. She was unable to move as the ball came closer and closer. She could hear the dogs' barking getting louder and louder. At the last moment, she fell to the ground, put her hands on her head, and hoped for the best.

There was a deafening whoosh followed by a soft plop noise. Then there was a humming that gradually decreased as the object travelled away into the distance, quieter and quieter, till there was no sound at all except for the scrambling of dogs trying to get up.

Lifting her head, Yuka stared into the sky to see the round object flying way off to the right. It must have swung away at the last moment, and Yuka could only sigh in relief. She stood up and went to straighten the dogs in their harnesses and undo all the criss-crossed lines. When she got to the front, Kikitu was standing still. His focus was directed off to the right, and he was sniffing and staring in that direction.

"What is it boy?" she asked, looking in the same direction.

"Something out there?" Yuka knew he could not answer but asked the question anyway.

Kikitu was distracted and kept pointing his head in that direction. He turned to her for a moment before turning back. Then he tried to move towards it, but he was held back by the harness.

"Okay, let's see what it is." Yuka stood up. "Hike,

Hike." She waited till the sled came by her and hopped on.

They followed the big dog's lead, but only had to move a short distance before they pulled up in front of something sticking out of the snow. Yuka jumped off the back of the sled and ran to the front to find a pair of black boots emerging from the snow. They wiggled about in the air.

"Is that what I think it is? Whose legs are they?" She was astounded.

Grabbing a leg, she pulled. From the black boots came red legs, then a red coat, and finally a red face with a white hair and beard that was shaking snow off in showers.

"Ho, Ho, that was fun flying through the air like that. It's a good job the snow was soft. I could have hurt myself."

"Santa, what are you doing here? Was that your sleigh that whizzed by?"

"Yes, it was my sleigh, and it turned so sharp that I fell out. I forgot to fasten the seat belt, you know. Now I am in trouble. Mrs. Claus will be very annoyed when I get back."

"But Santa, shouldn't you be getting ready for Christmas? It's very close, and you are...are...far from home."

The big guy stood up and shook off some more snow from his clothes. He looked around to get his bearings.

"Ho, no! I am in trouble." He stomped back and forth. His gaze went north, east, south, west, and back to north again. "I don't remember being here before, but I must have. I know everybody's houses all over the world. Are there houses near here?"

Yuka looked to the west. "My village is that way, but it's a couple of hours walk away."

"Oh, ho, no! Mrs. Claus is going to be extremely upset with me."

"How will you get back? Will the reindeer come back for you?"

"Only Rudolph knows how to find me; the others only know the way home. Mrs. Claus will be very irritated when they get home and I am not there. I left Rudolph back at the stables."

"Why?"

"He had a cough. I need him well for the big day, so I gave him some medication and let him rest."

"Does no one else know how to find you? Don't you have GPS, a smart phone, a satellite phone, or something like that?"

The red face got even redder. Santa looked around for an answer or perhaps for someone to blame.

"Well," he flustered and blustered, "I do have one, but I never took the time to learn how to use it. And I...mm...mm...forgot to bring the phone with me."

"Santa, everyone is relying on you. All the children are waiting for presents. What will you do if you cannot get going on time? Can you delay Christmas?" Yuka had a million questions.

"Don't panic me, young lady, I have to think."

Santa began wandering around in circles and speaking his thoughts out loud. "Now, when the sleigh gets back, Jessica – that's Mrs. Claus – will summon a meeting of the elves. They will question the reindeer, who will not know where I am. Next, they will organize a search party and send out the snowmobile squad. Since they don't know which way to go, they will spread out in all directions. Jessica will then call on Skoop the snowy owl and instruct him to find me. He will be the fastest and best bet to find me. I do hope they find me quickly."

Listening to all this made Yuka consider another alternative. She went to the sled and pulled out some snowshoes. Santa looked at her.

"That won't work my dear. I could not walk that far or quick enough."

"They are not for you, Santa. They are for me. I am going to walk the rest of the way home."

"Why?" The big guy asked.

"Because if anyone or anything can get you home fast, it is Kikitu. He and the rest of the team are the fastest sled dogs around."

"But they don't know the way," Santa stated.

"No, but I will point him north, and he will find

the way. He is your best bet – at least until others find you."

"I don't know," he mused.

"Santa, get in," Yuka ordered Santa in a light-hearted way. She held up the blankets on the sled.

"Are you sure?"

"Yes!" she said. "The commands for the dogs are "Hike" to go, "Whoa" to stop, "Gee" to go right, and "Haw" to go left. You will only need to say stop or go, because if you don't know the way, then Kikitu must find it."

"If you are sure, I guess this is my best option." Reluctantly Santa stepped into the sled and sat down.

Yuka covered him with the blankets and tucked him in. She wanted to make sure he would be snug and warm on the journey. She pulled out a thermos that had been hooked onto the sled guide rails.

"Here is a drink for when you are thirsty. It is *suaasat*, a traditional soup. Sorry, it's not milk."

"Ho, Ho! That's a myth. I really like a cup of tea. But you cannot expect people to leave a hot drink by the cookies, now can you?"

The girl walked along the line making sure the harness for each dog was hitched correctly. When she reached the front, she knelt down and put her arms around the lead dog's neck.

"Kik, you must get Santa to the North Pole as soon as possible, or children all over the world will not get their presents. Then there would be lots and lots of tears and some very upset mums and dads. She pointed north. "I can only tell you it's that way, but how far I do not know. Now it is up to you."

She stood up, looked down the line, and towards Santa. There wasn't anything else she could do.

"Hike! Hike!" Go as fast as you can."

As the sled passed, she held out her hand. Santa gave her a "high five" with his white-gloved hand. Then he waved and said, "Thank you, Yuka. I will remember this."

She bent down to tie on her snowshoes. When she looked up, the sleigh was getting farther and farther away. She wished she could have gone with them, but she knew two passengers would be too heavy. She didn't want to slow them down.

When her shoes were nice and snug on her feet, she stood up just in time to see the sled disappear over a hill and drop down out of sight. Then she turned towards home.

CHAPTER TWO

Faster and faster, Kikitu spurted ahead. He was driven by the will to do his job and get Santa home. Snow flew from his feet and showered the dogs behind, making them growl in discontent.

"Slow down," they called to the leader. "We cannot keep up. You are going too fast, and the pace will kill us all."

He knew they were right, so he slowed to a run. He took most of the load himself as he stretched out the rope from his shoulders. Tongues fell out of open mouths again as each dog ran to the limit of his or her endurance. On and on they pulled through a white sea of endless wilderness.

"You are going the wrong way!" one dog called from the back. "North is to the left."

"No, to the right," another shouted.

"It is this way," Kikitu declared. "Faster! We must go faster to save Christmas."

"We cannot go faster," said Sitka, the other lead dog beside him.

Kikitu held the pace and tried to take more of the strain. "We have to keep going as fast as we can. One at a time, each of you take the load off and run free for a while. Get back your breath. Let's start at the back. Fluff you go first."

Fluff got his name from his fluffy hair that made him look like a cottony, bubbly ball of wool. When he lay down in the snow, others snuggled up to him to get warm in his bundle of fur.

After a while Kikitu called out again. "Your turn, Zaria."

Zaria was a quiet dog who liked to sit and watch the other dogs play. She was not lazy, but she liked to watch the others chase a stick around and try to grab it in their mouth to be the "one".

Next was Neo whose name meant "the one". He always had to catch the stick and run around while the others tried to grab it. But he would swivel, swing, and jump to avoid losing the stick.

Taeko's name meant "game" and he really was game for anything! He would chase Neo until he got the stick and then run hard and fast around the dogs playing the game.

Then came Granite's turn. The big grey dog had a lot of wolf blood in him. This made him strong and tough like a solid block of stone.

Before Sitka, the other lead dog, had a turn to ease off, it was Blazer who took the load off his shoulders and spun his legs in an easy run. He was also known as "Trail Blazer".

"I think you are leading us the wrong way," said Blazer. "Off to the right is north. I feel it in my bones."

It was well known he also could find his way home when others were lost.

"No, I believe we are on the right track," Kikitu declared. "We must keep going before it gets dark, and we cannot see the way."

Light snow started to fall, making the way ahead harder to see, but they kept pushing on. Kikitu would not allow them to slow down. Mile after mile, the landscape ahead did not change. All they could see was an endless vista of snow in uneven low hills. Up and down they went. Up and down till a silver fox appeared from behind a hillock. It trotted along at the side of the dogs. Its little legs had to go at twice the speed of the bigger animals.

"Where are you going, Kikitu, in such a hurry?" he asked, twisting his head to look at the leader.

"Taking Santa to the North Pole, Floop, for he is lost. Now go away for I do not have time for you right now," the leader answered.

Santa's head popped up above the blankets, listening.

"But you are going the wrong way," the fox said. "It is way to this side, and you are going away from it."

"No, it is straight ahead. Now leave us alone." Kikitu barked and snapped at the heels of the fox, making it veer away. It slowed to a walk and called after them.

"I think I will follow you because when you drop dead, I will have lots to eat. That is, unless the white bear gets you first!"

Kikitu ignored the fox and set his sights on a dark mound up ahead. As they got closer, they could see a bulbous shape lying on the snow next to a hole. It was the seal, Frieda.

"Hold up, Kikitu, where are you going at such speed?" the seal called out at their approach. The travellers slowed to a walk, and most of the dogs gasped to get their breath and a short rest.

"We are taking Santa to the North Pole because he fell from his sleigh."

Santa's head popped up from under the blankets. He was listening and curious to know why they had stopped.

"You are going the wrong way," the seal stated. "It is back the way you came."

"No, it is forward."

"No, back that way."

"No, forward," the large dog insisted.

"Back."

"I know for sure it is forward. Now, Frieda, do not hinder us for we are in a hurry." Kikitu jumped forward, dragging the pack to a run again. As they sped past the hole in the ice for the seal, Frieda slipped back into her natural realm.

Kikitu veered a little to the left to get back on solid ground. No one spoke for they were breathless and panting so hard it was impossible to make a sound.

Now the leader drove on harder and faster. From a distance, they looked like a huge ball of swirling snow rolling along the white wasteland.

One dog fell, and there was panic as the other dogs fell over each other. The sled slowed to a stop with a mangled heap of animals in front.

"Get up!" Kikitu commanded. "Get up!"

"We cannot go any further," a dog called from the bottom of the pile.

"You are killing us," another complained.

Sitka, who was almost the size of Kikitu, stood up in front of the leader and threatened him.

"If you do not slow down, I will take over."

The large white dog pounced on top of the other dog. He grabbed him by the throat, then pinned him down before growling in his ear.

"You will do as I say, or I will cut you loose and leave you for the white bear!"

Santa popped his head over the blankets.

"Now, now, boys. No squabbling. There is no need for bullying here. I will not stand for it."

"You can hear us talking?" Kikitu was amazed.

"Yes, I can, but then I am Santa and can talk to most animals. Now stop any more arguing and take a rest."

There was an enormous sigh of relief, and most lay down to take a mouthful of snow to quench their thirst. Kikitu went around and turned dogs to untangle the harnesses till they were all straight.

"Santa, do you know where we are?"

Santa stared at the stars and seemed to be making some mental calculations. Then he checked the stars again.

"No," he replied.

Kiki's head dropped in disappointment.

"We just have to keep going till we come across the way home. I seem to remember an *inuksuk* close by. If we come to it, I think we can find the way from there."

They rested for a short time, and Santa took a drink from the thermos. The dogs were content with snow.

"It's not nice hot tea, but soup is good anytime."

Kikitu did not want to waste anymore time and soon stood up.

"We need to get going. Everyone up!"

The team stood and shook the snow out of their fur. Then they set off once again at a steady trot. This time, they tried not to race or tire themselves out. They moved at a constant pace for kilometre after kilometre.

Seeing a white mound ahead, Kikitu set his sights on it. Closer and closer they came. Then, when they almost reached it, the mound moved and a huge white bear reared up and stood on its hind legs! It bared its huge white teeth in a loud snarl.

The pack skidded to a halt. Legs flailed, as the dogs all tried to get away from the massive animal that stood in their way. They looked to Kikitu for direction.

"Where are you going, Kikitu?" the bear roared. His mouth and teeth gaped open in a threatening display.

"Let us pass, Tatuk, for I do not wish to fight you

again. Santa needs to get back to the North Pole before Christmas or there will be no Christmas or presents for anyone."

"But Kikitu," the bear laughed, "you are going the wrong way. The North Pole is over that way." He pointed with his head, but Kikitu knew Tatuk was lying for he could smell the sea.

"Thank you, great Tatuk, for you are wise. I will take that way if you let me pass."

"Certainly," the bear said and dropped to his four paws and moved away. He smiled for he thought he had a feast before him without a fight. He had only to follow them till they dropped through thin ice.

The white dog kept his eyes on the bear as he turned towards the sea and broke into a run. When they were a little distance away, he suddenly veered back to his original path. A loud roar rang out behind, and Kikitu guessed Tatuk was angry at being tricked. But

Kikitu had no time to waste and ran on.

Through swirling clouds of snow, Kikitu could see the path ahead narrowed between two high mounds. Then it ran downward to a track that was just barely wide enough for the sled. Somehow, he knew this was the way to go, but he could smell trouble ahead. The rest of the team could smell it too for their noses were as keen as Kikitu's.

"There is danger ahead," Sitka stated.

"I know. I smell them as well. I just hope they do not stop us."

Long before they got there, the team could tell that a group of muskoxen were ahead. Their noses even told them there were ten adults and two young- sters. Sure enough, they soon appeared as black and brown shadows in the mist, and they blocked the path.

The muskoxen were gathered in a circle. Their hindquarters were back to back, so they could protect the smaller ones in the middle. Their large, long, curved horns pointed straight at the oncoming sled. Their coats were a mix of black, grey, and brown, and their hair almost reached the ground. This is why the Inuit called them *umingmak*, the bearded ones.

The team came to a halt, as they had no choice. Kikitu slipped out of his harness to approach them.

"What do you want?" a deep, gruff voice called out. "You cannot have our young ones!"

"We only want to pass, Oomanuuk. We wish you no harm. Do you know the way to the North Pole?"

"So, you know my name. Well, I know yours too, Kikitu the Amaruk. No one touches our calves."

A large dominant female, who was the leader of the herd, stepped forward. She pawed the ground with her large front hoof and then dropped her head to make a charge.

"No, no, wait!" Kikitu urged. "We need to get Santa to the North Pole, or there will be no Christmas."

"Santa? Who is Santa?" The muskoxen asked.

"I am Santa." A voice came from the back of the sled, and Santa stood up and stepped out.

"Oomanuuk, we have never met, but I know of you." Santa began walking towards the muskox and dog who were confronting each other. "Your kind goes back to ancient times when you saw animals who are no longer with us. But you still remain, so know me as a friend and let us pass."

Santa walked straight up to the beast and stroked her head. He ran his hand along her long coat and then put his head next to hers.

"See, I have a beard too." He pulled his hand through the white hair. "Ho, Ho. Ho." Then without asking, he walked amongst the herd gently stroking them and whispering in their ears. They gradually parted in the middle to make enough room for the sled.

Kikitu slipped back into the harness and quietly, slowly, the dogs walked through the herd. The muskoxen sniffed and snorted as they passed by. The dogs eyed them warily.

With Santa back in the sled, they carried on. But the snow began falling harder. Heavier and thicker it came down. Then the wind got up and blew into their faces. It was hard to see, yet Kikitu pushed on. Soon the others started complaining.

"We are lost."

"I cannot see. We must stop till the storm blows past."

"The path is not there. We need to find the way."

"Follow me!" the Kikitu, the leader, called back. "I know the way."

But truth be told, he did not know the way! His heart was sad that he might let them down, but determination drove him on. He strained, taking all the load himself to allow the others to keep pace.

The storm grew and worsened till they were completely blinded. This forced them to slow down to a walk. But still Kiki pulled the load, ready to do anything to get Santa home and fulfill Yuka's wish.

Silently, he closed his eyes. His heart sought the way, and his mind fought for the will power to keep going. Then a voice spoke to him.

"Kikitu, you must not give up. You cannot give up."

"Waruk, is that you? We thought you were dead."
Kikitu turned to look in the direction of the voice,
but saw nothing. But when he squinted, he could
see a ghostly outline of a wolf walking beside him.
then it disappeared.

"You are the strongest of us and can do it," the
voice spoke again. Then the voice and the wolf
shape disappeared.

Stories of the great northern wolf had been told for
years. Kikitu had heard all the tales of Waruk and
his battles with Mahaha who stole children and
tickled them to death.. It was said the white wolf
had accompanied great hunters who fought the evil
Ljiraat, shape shifters who could change into any
animal but could not hide their red eyes.

A great battle had been fought against the Inupasugjuk
giants, and it was said Waruk the great had been
vanquished. Now Kikitu believed he had heard the

voice. It lifted his spirits and strengthened his will.

At last he opened his deep blue eyes and focused forward, seeking a place to stop. The team needed to rest, as they were almost ready to give up. Suddenly, a dark shape appeared out of the gloom. It appeared angular and had "arms" jutting out. As they got closer, he knew the shape and was glad he had found the inuksuk.

CHAPTER THREE

The gloom around the inuksuk seemed to lighten as they got nearer. Huge, oblong, black stones stuck out from a dark body, like arms pointing the way. Perched on one of the arms was a snowy owl with large yellow eyes. Kikitu pulled up close to it so all could see. Santa popped his head out from underneath the blankets.

"Skoop, you found us," Santa said happily.

"Yeses, wheoot have you been till noooow?" the owl tweeted.

"Coming, that's where we've been. We've been coming as quick as we can."

"Mrs. Claus is wreally ma, veery, veery mad. You have to get home as quickly as possible. The sleigh is packed. Rudolf and the reindeer are all wready, and you have to leeeve tonight."

"I know. I know. You don't have to tell me! How about you tell the pack and Kikitu about Christmas Island. They need to see the way, so take this pouch of starlight dust." Santa fiddled in his jacket and pulled out a red velvet pouch and held it up. "And sprinkle them."

The owl swooped down, took the pouch, and flew up and down the line, emptying the dust over the top of the dogs. It sparkled and shone in the gloom and gave them all glistening diamond coats that twinkled, flickered, and glimmered in the darkness. Finally, the owl landed by Kikitu and began the explanation.

"Santa's woorkshop, his grotto where he stoores all

the tooys, the stables for the reindeer, and all the hooses where the elves live are on a hidden island at the North Pole. "Christmas Island" is what we call it. There is anoother Christmas Island where big people live and some of oour mail is sent there, but the elves regularly fetch it all to be soorted. Sometimes Santa visits there for his summer holidays and stays near Flying Fish Cove.

"A shield coovers our island to keep it secret. If you loooked there, all you would only see is a lot of water. So yoou need the dust so yoou can see it and journey to it."

Skoop stopped for a moment and swivelled his head from side to side. It looked like he had turned his head all the way around in a full circle. His large staring eyes locked onto the dogs.

"How did you do that?" Kikitu asked.

"Doo what? I thought I had heard something, but it

was just the wind, and it is getting stronger. Listen, I will fly in froont of yoou till we get near the sea, and froom there, you can see the island. Then I will leave yoou to get there on yoour oown while I summon back all the search parties. Goot that?"

"Got it," Kikitu replied.

"Oone more thing. When yoou get on the ice, yoou will have to move fast because it is thin. If you sloow doon, you may fall through. Sooo, if you hear some cracking nooises, do noot let it bother yoou.

"Keep gooing till you reach the island. Yoou will see a road lined with Christmas lights and that will guide you right intoo town. The sleigh is hooused in the middle of the toown square."

"Right, got that," Kikitu said.

With that, the owl took off, swung around the inuksuk, and veered off in a northerly direction.

The sled moved off with a lurch, and Santa settled back down into the warm blankets.

They trotted along, keeping pace with the owl flying low in front of them. Spirits were now lifted and legs and bodies moved happily as the dogs felt their destination was near.

Skoop dropped down over a slight hill. As the team also went over, they saw that the path was down-hill. At the bottom, the sea spread out in sheets of ice before them. In the distance, lights glowed in all different colours.

Kikitu was elated at the sight. Only a short time before, he had been ready to give up, but now the end was in sight. The owl swooped low beside him.

"Yoou can see the lights? Yes?" Skoop asked.

"Yes."

"Goo for it! I have to call back the search parties. Doon't foorget what I said and keep moving on the ice." With that, he took off into the air and disappeared behind them.

They began going faster and faster downhill as the sled slid quicker and quicker. By the time they hit the ice, they were going faster than ever before.

But on the ice, paws slipped and legs started to go one way or the other. They tried to use the claws on their paws to dig in, but their constant running had worn them down so they could not grip the ice. Panic started to control their movements and the sleigh and pack slowed down and began to sway and slide from side to side. Santa's head bobbed up, and he assessed the situation.

"Steady! You reindeer - sorry - dogs, don't worry. Settle down, and we will be okay. KIKITU! You keep us headed towards the lights, and the rest of you listen to me."

He started to shout out commands: "Gee" and then "Haw". Getting them to go one way, and then the other, Santa gradually got the sled straightened up. They had slowed down a lot, and the pace needed to quicken.

"Hike! Hike!" he called out. "But easy and steadily." The dogs understood him and did their best to gain speed again. Kikitu just focused on the lights and headed straight towards them.

Everything was nice and easy until they were halfway across the ice. Then they heard a cracking noise. It was quiet, but still a cracking sound. Kikitu closed his ears to the noise and just focused on the far side and the bright lights that meant safety. The noise got louder, then louder still. Santa looked back to see a wash of open water behind them. The back of the sled was sinking!

"Hike! Hike!" he cried. "Faster! We must go faster."

Kikitu leaned harder into the harness around his shoulders and spurred the others to go harder too. But exhaustion had taken its toll. Most of the other dogs were so tired that it was a struggle to keep going. The lead dogs tried hard to encourage more speed. Sitka found a second wind and also leaned into his harness. Together they hit the ice in unison, front paws together, and then hind legs digging in. The speed increased. Santa looked back and muttered to himself.

"Oh, no! We are so close, we cannot fail now." The sea behind them was opening up as if to swallow them, and he had a sinking feeling. "Hike! Kikitu, hike!"

The shoreline on the other side seemed so close

yet so out of reach. Kikitu had no more to give. His heart was beating so fast, and his breathing was out of control as he tried to suck in more air. He focused on the road on the island and thought he saw lights coming towards them. He blinked to make sure. There were definitely lights speeding towards them! What were they?

Santa called out. "It's the snowmobile squad coming to help us!"

Reaching the ice, two sets of three snowmobiles veered in opposite directions and turned in a big loop to come alongside the sled. Each snowmobile had two riders wearing green snowsuits and red crash helmets. The snow machines were smaller than normal because they were made for elves. As they drew next to the sled, the rear passengers threw loops of rope over to the sled. The dogs could do nothing but keep on running, but Santa grabbed them and tied them to the side of the sled.

Once they were secure, the snowmobiles sped up and took the load off the dogs so they could run faster. There was hardly any ice on top of the sea, and the machines were water-cross skipping on top of the sea, dragging the dog team and sled to land.

Soon they skimmed up onto land and slowed down. The machines eased up till they all came to a stop. Then the rear riders jumped off and retrieved the ropes and talked to Santa.

One lifted the visor on his helmet. "Are you okay, Santa? What about the dogs? Are they alright?"

"Yes, yes, we are all thankful we made it." Santa let out a huge sigh of relief.

"Mrs. Claus is waiting for you at the stables, and everything is ready to go. The only thing is... she is not very happy." The elf's voice was very chirpy and high pitched.

"That bad?"

"Yes, but at least you will be able to make the run," the chipper voice said.

"Kikitu, it is not much further. Do you think you and the team can go just a little further?"

CHAPTER FOUR

Tired but happy, the dogs trotted along at a steady pace. Their tongues hung out as they usually did along the trail. After only a couple of minutes, houses appeared on the edge of town. They could see lights strung out from building to building in a bright corridor directing their way.

Escorted on both sides by snowmobiles, the sled team hit the streets to loud cheers from elves lining the streets. The whole village had come out to greet them and see them home. Loud singing and applause came from all around. As they passed by, elves dropped in behind them. The men were dressed in green suits with furry white collars and trim. The women were dressed in the same colour

but had wide skirts down to their ankles. Some had baby elves strapped to their backs or carried them in front on a sling.

The throng grew bigger and bigger as they went along. They were very noisy. The elves jumped up and down and skipped along, calling out at the same time:

"Hey, ho, along we go.

Santa's back through all that snow.

Rescued by the dogs of men.

Stories we will write with pen.

Of Christmas saved again."

Santa was waving to them. "Ho, ho, good to see you all, ho, ho, ho."

Sitka turned his head to Kikitu. "Have you ever

seen such a happy bunch?"

"No, but I think they are glad that all the toys they made this year are going to be delivered on time."

"Guess so."

They turned a corner into the town square. There was a huge building right in the middle with big double doors that were wide open, doors on the other side were also open like a drive through. The sign above the doors read: "Sleigh Barn and Stables." In the middle of the building, stood the sleigh filled with parcels and presents. In front, the reindeers were hitched up and ready to go. Their heads turned back looking for their driver.

The toy workshops were on both sides of the street. Covered chutes led from the buildings to either side of the sleigh barn. They conveyed parcels and toys and goodies straight onto the sleigh along conveyor belts and slides.

Kikitu guided their sled right up to the steps on one side of the barn. He saw a woman standing at the top, wearing a red coat, a long green skirt, and a white fake fur hat to keep warm. She was not smiling or laughing and looked stern.

Elves jumped around the sled undoing the harness and letting the dogs out. Although the dogs wanted to skip around with the elves, they were too exhausted. Granite started licking one of the elves on the face.

"Hey, these guys taste like chocolate," he said and began licking again. That started all the dogs licking the elves' faces. This made the elves giggle with glee. Before long, dogs and elves were tumbling and stumbling all over each other. They laughed, chuckled, sniggered, and chortled as they rolled in a ball of bodies, legs, and paws.

Quietness descended, and they all looked up to see Santa climbing the stairs. He approached Mrs. Claus and went to kiss her on the cheek, but she stepped back from him.

"Where have you been?" she asked with a stern face.

"I was coming home as quickly as I could. I had a slight accident."

"Accident, accident! What sort of accident?"

"I took the reindeer out to stretch their legs. They had been inside so long, and they needed a run. But when I did a tight turn to come home, the sleigh tilted and I fell out."

"Didn't the seat belt hold you in?"

Santa looked around in embarrassment, trying to find an excuse. "No."

"Why not?" she demanded.

"I forgot to fasten it."

"And the GPS?"

"Forgot it."

"And your satellite phone?"

"Forgot it," he said sheepishly.

"You have been naughty. Do you know what that means?"

"Honey bee, it was an accident."

"Don't you 'honey bee' me. You were neglectful, negligent, and...naughty!"

"Sweet pea, I did not mean for it to happen. I got here as fast as I could, thanks to the dogs."

"Sweet pea, sweet pea, never you mind the cute names. You were... **Naughty**! Because I am the only one who can give you presents, that means you might not be getting anything this year."

"But...but."

"Never mind the 'buts'. You had better get going. You are already two minutes late. If you have not eaten, that's your fault. You will just have to fill up with milk and cookies."

Santa turned to the crowd, his head bowed. "Got to go. Thanks everyone for getting ready for this night. Kikitu and the team, rest up. The elves will feed you. Get some sleep, and when I have finished, I will take you home in the sleigh. You got me here, so the least I can do is get you home."

With that he turned, walked to the sleigh, and stepped in. "Ho! ho! This is the best night of the year, let's go."

The elves started chanting:

"Hey ho away he flies.
Into the night, he flies, he cries,
'Ho, ho, ho!'
Santa knows who is naughty or nice,
Presents they get whatever the price.
Christmas, is a time to give."

A white velvet hand raised up in the air, and Santa waved to all as the sleigh moved forward, sped up, and burst through the far exit door and up into the air. Everyone watched till he was out of sight.

Quiet singing began as the elves moved away and went back to their homes. The dogs were approached by Mrs. Claus.

"Thank you for all you have done. Skoop told me all about it. You really have saved Christmas."

Kikitu spoke up. "Mrs. Claus, will Santa not get any presents at all?"

"Of course, he will, but I had to tell him off because he is always being reckless. Last year he got into trouble with a fighter plane that thought he was a UFO. It chased him all the way to Australia, and Santa was playing with it by swerving, diving, and flying all over the place. He got in trouble because he had no satellite phone to tell them who he was."

"That's good. I thought he of all people should get a present."

"Call me Jessica," said Mrs. Claus, and she smiled. "I have a box of his favourite tea, a bag of his favourite cookies, and chocolate-covered oatmeal flapjacks for him. I also got him a new GPS transceiver, which I will stitch into his jacket so we can always find him, and a new phone to install in the sleigh. Plus I got him a new automatic seat belt system that closes around him as soon as he sits down."

The dogs all chuckled. "I guess you will not need us again then," one said.

"Hopefully not, but you never know. Now the elves will feed you, and you can sleep in the barns or out in the snow if you want. I know you are used to sleeping in the snow. I am off home now to get ready for his return. Goodnight."

"Goodnight, Jessica," the dogs called back.

After being fed, most slept in the barn snuggled up to Fluff, but Kikitu preferred the outside. He found a bank of snow and turned around and around in a circle to make a bed. He settled down with his head on his paws and looked up at the sky.

The night had cleared and ribbons of colours danced in waves overtop the landscape, bathing it in rays of reds, green, yellows, and blue. Feeling contented, he closed his eyes and fell asleep thinking of Yuka.

CHAPTER FIVE

But Yuka was NOT asleep. There was no way she could get to sleep, lying in bed in her grandfather's house, surrounded by all her family. All she could do was worry. What had happened to her sled dog team? Was Kikitu okay or did he have to fight the great white bear again? Would Christmas be ruined? Would nobody get any presents? She wished she had gone with them.

Hundreds of questions ran through her head and sleep was impossible. She listened as hard as she could. Maybe she would hear Santa coming, and she could ask him what happened. But she did not know that Santa dropped sleeping dust before entering a house, so no one would ever see him. So it was that Yuka finally fell asleep.

Loud shouting woke her up. The sun was streaming through the window. She jumped up and gazed out at a bright sunny day. Children were outside, and they were playing with toys. They were playing with *new* toys! Her heart jumped for joy. Santa had been here, and so Christmas had been saved. She danced around the room, jumping up and down, and occasionally going back to the window to make sure it was not a dream. After getting dressed, she ran downstairs to find the family unwrapping presents, drinking warm beverages, and chatting noisily.

"There you are, sleepy head," her grandfather stated. "I thought you said Christmas might be late this year, if it came at all."

She smiled. "Looks like I was wrong, doesn't it?"

He gave her a knowing smile of understanding. "Your dogs did well then."

"Guess so."

"Guess what?" one of her nephews asked.

"Guess you are all happy Santa has been here!"

"Sure are! Would you like to play a video game with me? You can be the villain. I will be Batman."

"Can I open my presents first?"

"Okay," he replied, turning his attention back to his new game.

Yuka unwrapped her presents to find she had received a small camping stove to heat food on the trail and a new camouflage sleeping bag. She just loved being outdoors.

Next, there was a pair of mukluks and a matching pair of mitts to keep her warm. There was also a box with her name clearly marked on it. Underneath, it said: "From Santa." She carefully opened the paper to find a satellite phone with a letter. Hurriedly she read it:

Dear Yuka,

Thank you so much for your help and saving Christmas from being a disaster.

I cannot tell you how much I appreciated your aid. I am sure if the boys and girls of the world knew what you and your team of dogs had done, they would be thankful too.

*As a special gift, I have given you this satellite phone. My number is in your contact list and is number one on your speed dial file. **Please do not give it out!!!!** Otherwise, the whole world will be phoning me.*

I will be taking my usual week's rest, after the big day. I will call you after that. You never know when I might need your help again. I will catch up with all your news then.

Best regards,

Santa

P.S. Jessica (Mrs. Claus) sends her thanks. She says she is sorry she never got to meet you, but she loves your dogs.

"Grandad, Grandad! Yuka called out. "Santa has given me a phone, look."

She gave the letter and phone to her grandfather, and he examined them carefully.

"Is this in exchange for Kikitu, the sled, and the rest of the dogs?"

"NO!" she exclaimed. "He cannot have my team! I only let him borrow them. This must be our secret. You haven't told anyone have you? I only told you because I came home without the dogs."

"Joking. I am only joking with you. I will not tell anyone." He smiled at her. "You must be the only person to have a direct line to the Big Guy." He handed the letter back to her.

"This just goes to show that if you help someone, not only do they want to pay you back, they want to be your friend as well." He winked at her and joked, "Can you put in a good word for me?"

Yuka was overjoyed and spent most of the day going around to all of her relatives to get their phone numbers and put them in her contact list. She promised to call them regularly when out on the trail.

CHAPTER SIX

Santa had been gone a long time. Kikitu and the rest of the dogs had woken up and wandered around the village. Many of the elves had called them over to feed them and thank them again.

Everyone was relaxed and glad all the work they had done was over for now. There was time for a short rest before beginning again.

Kikitu talked to one of the elves. "Santa has been gone a long time. Do you think he is alright?"

"Of course, he is fine. Don't forget, he has to go through all the time zones. He starts in the continent of Australia and New Zealand and works through their night. Then he moves to the continent of Asia, delivering all through their night. Then he is up into Europe before he moves to Africa then the Americas. Thankfully, he has only a couple of stops in Antarctica. So you see, he does not work though one night, but many people's nights. But don't worry, he will be home soon.

The dogs wandered around and ended up walking into the workshops to find some elves were working.

"What are you doing working? We thought you all were resting."

"Oh no," one replied. "We have a special project that Mrs. Claus asked us to do."

The elves moved apart to reveal the dogs' own sled was being renovated. The elves had put on new runners, new rails, and a new seat that folded out into a bed. In fact, it looked like everything was brand new.

"Wow. It's like new," Sitka said.

"Yes," the elf replied. "And look, we have added a new harness for each of you with padding around the shoulders to ease the burden."

"Wow," they all said together, walking around the sled and examining it.

"We have to hurry," the elf stated. "Santa will be back soon. Return to the barn while we finish up."

When they arrived at the barn, Jessica was already there, preparing for the sleigh's arrival.

"Good, you are all back in time. Santa will be here soon. I talked to him on his phone, and he has finished his deliveries and is coming home. I made sure his phone was in the sleigh before it left."

The elves arrived, pulling their sled into the barn. It was all bright and new looking.

"Thank you for repairing the sled," Kikitu said.

"And for the new harness," Sitka also stated.

"You're welcome!" Jessica smiled and turned her head abruptly. "I hear him coming."

Elves, dogs, and woman stared into the sky where a bright shiny light started to become larger and larger. Soon they could make out the shape of reindeer, a sleigh, and Santa.

It swung around in a loop to come in straight and true through the entrance. There was a whoosh as it entered the barn and came to a stop. The reindeer were all panting and shaking their heads.

Immediately, the elves starting loading the dog sled into the middle of the sleigh and removing bags from the back. Santa did not get out. Instead he motioned the dogs to get in. Mrs. Claus stepped up, and they kissed each other on the cheek.

"What are the bags you are taking out of the sleigh?" Kikitu asked one of the elves.

"Those are full of cookies," he replied. "Santa cannot eat all the cookies left out for him so he brings some home – especially the best ones made by the children themselves. Then next week, we have an elves' tea and cookie party and Santa tells us stories of his journeys.

Then we sing songs to Mr. and Mrs. Claus. We even have a dance. The funniest part is when Santa gets up to do the chicken dance. He flaps his elbows up and down and bobs his head. His beard falls forward and he looks like a chicken feeding. Mrs. Claus cannot dance because she is usually laughing so hard. We all fall on the floor laughing as well.'

The elf got serious for a moment. "This year we will sing a new song to honour snow dogs of the northern wilderness."

"That sounds great. I wish I could be there, but I have to go home."

The dogs all looked towards Jessica.

"Did it go alright?" she asked Santa.

"Fine, no troubles at all," he replied. "Might as well get the dogs home before I settle down for my week's rest."

"That is what I thought," Jessica replied.

"We always think alike you and I." He smiled at her and turned around. "Everybody in?"

Some elves were in the sleigh also to make sure the sled was fixed in properly.

"Seat belt on, Santa?" Mrs. Claus looked in to check.

"Ho, ho, ho, lets go Rudolph."

There was a jolt as they moved off, and the dogs

scrambled to get a hold and settle in. Mrs. Claus was waving to them as they lifted into the air. The dogs opened their mouths to suck in the wind as they sped up. Their joy was overwhelming as they skimmed over the sea and then over land.

Soon the sleigh descended onto a flat snow-packed area almost like a landing strip of an airport. The reindeer eased to a stop, and the dogs waited while the elves lifted out their sled. They were a little reluctant to get out because they had enjoyed their flight so much.

"Please all roll over in the snow," Santa said.

They were not sure why, but they did as they were told.

"Sorry, but we have to remove all the stardust so you will not be able to talk with humans anymore. The dust allowed you to talk with us and the elves. No such thing as talking dogs, is there? If I need you again, I will send Skoop with another pouch of dust."

After the elves hitched the dogs up to the sled in their new harness, he spoke again.

"Thank you all again for getting me home. Maybe next year I will teach you to fly, and you can be back up for the reindeer. Would you like that?"

Tails wagged, and they barked in unison.

"Your village is that way." He pointed, but they already knew the way. Then Santa went to each dog in turn and petted their heads and necks.

"Hike! Hike!" Santa called out one last time, and they took off down the trail.

Yuka was outside talking with her cousins when the team entered the village and ran straight to her. The dogs barked and yelped in excitement as she walked the line, rubbing their heads and petting them with loving affection.

"It's so good to see you all. I have missed you. Did you have a good time?"

"We have been to Christmas Island, seen the elves, the grotto, and workshop. We spoke to Jessica - Mrs. Claus, and saw the snowmobile squad, the reindeer, and everything," Kikitu and the other dogs said at the same time.

"Stop barking. I can see you all had a great adventure without me."

"She cannot understand us," Kikitu said to the others in disappointment.

Yuka went inside the house and emerged shortly after, dressed in new clothes, mitts, and mukluks. Then she loaded the sleigh with food and camping gear, and the family emerged to say goodbye.

"Off to seek more adventures?" Grandfather asked. "Don't forget to get back in time for school."

"I will, I will," She replied. "Hike! Hike!"

"Well, be careful." The family waved goodbye to her.

She waved to all her friends as she passed through the village.

As they sped into the wilderness, a snowy owl flew past, swooped around and up into the air, keeping watch over them on their travels.

PICTURE GLOSSARY

DOG SLED AND TEAM

SLED AND DOG HARNESS

SNOWMOBILE

82

SATELLITE PHONE

INUKSHUK (signpost)

G.P.S. TRANSCEIVER

AMAUTI women's parka with built in baby pouch

MITTS

YUKA'S CLOTHING

SNOWY OWL

83

MUKLUKS

INUKSUK marker of sacred and special places

NOTE

If you want more information on Items in the story then search the internet using...

Keywords like...

- Inuit Mythology
- Inukshuk or Inuksuk *(both have same meaning and have different uses can you find them?)*
- Mukluks
- Snowmobiles, Sleds etc.
- Arctic Animals
- Amaruk
- Komatik

Acknowledgements

Special thanks to Natalie
For suggestions, critique and encouragement.

 FriesenPress

Suite 300 - 990 Fort St
Victoria, BC, V8V 3K2
Canada

www.friesenpress.com

Copyright © 2018 by Tommy Conner
First Edition — 2018

ISBN
978-1-5255-2664-0 (Hardcover)
978-1-5255-2665-7 (Paperback)
978-1-5255-2666-4 (eBook)

1. JUVENILE FICTION, HOLIDAYS & CELEBRATIONS, CHRISTMAS & ADVENT

Distributed to the trade by The Ingram Book Company

CPSIA information can be obtained
at www.ICGtesting.com
Printed in the USA
LVHW07s0719020918
588916LV00001B/1/P